This book belongs to

_____

_____

Look out for other Piccolo and Annabelle books:

A Very Messy Inspection
A Disastrous Party

Piccolo and Annabelle
VOLUME THREE

THE STINKY CHEESE
GYPSIES

WRITTEN AND ILLUSTRATED BY

STEPHEN AXELSEN

OXFORD
UNIVERSITY PRESS

OXFORD
UNIVERSITY PRESS

Great Clarendon Street, Oxford OX2 6DP

Oxford University Press is a department of the University of Oxford.
It furthers the University's objective of excellence in research, scholarship,
and education by publishing worldwide in

Oxford   New York

Auckland   Cape Town   Dar es Salaam   Hong Kong   Karachi
Kuala Lumpur   Madrid   Melbourne   Mexico City   Nairobi
New Delhi   Shanghai   Taipei   Toronto

With offices in

Argentina   Austria   Brazil   Chile   Czech Republic   France   Greece
Guatemala   Hungary   Italy   Japan   Poland   Portugal   Singapore
South Korea   Switzerland   Thailand   Turkey   Ukraine   Vietnam

Oxford is a registered trade mark of Oxford University Press
in the UK and in certain other countries

First published 2005 by Random House Australia Pty Ltd, Sydney, Australia.
This edition published by arrangement with Random House Australia.

First published in the UK in 2006

British Library Cataloguing in Publication Data

Data available

ISBN-13: 978-0-19-272611-7
ISBN-10: 0-19-272611-0

1 3 5 7 9 10 8 6 4 2

Printed in Great Britain by Mackays of Chatham plc, Chatham, Kent

For Harlee, a true gentleman.

CONTENTS

Holywell, No. 9 Pleasant Crescent

CHAPTER ONE
An Embarrassment of Riches

'We've been robbed! Again!' cried Annabelle.

'Good,' said Piccolo Grande, 'we have far too much stuff.'

His great-aunt dropped her shopping bags on the driveway and ran about frantically.

'My beautiful gnomes! Gone! And my grand piano!'

'At least we can get in the front door now,' humphed Piccolo.

This was their second burglary of the week, and the fifth of the month. Not so long ago,

Piccolo would have been horrified by a single burglary. But these were unusual times. Times had been unusual, strange, and odd ever since Great-Aunt Annabelle had come to stay.

Piccolo had been living all alone in his beautiful big house, content in his own company. He was a peace-loving and orderly boy, and it had been a quiet and predictable life. The dishes were always done, his socks were always folded in neat rows in the drawer marked 'socks'. The lid of the toothpaste was always neatly closed.

But a dark cloud was hanging over Piccolo's carefully combed head. His parents had vanished. Twenty-four months ago Marjorie and Peter Grande had sailed into a thick tropical mist and disappeared. Not a soul had seen them since. Piccolo was sure they would be found, and there would be a blissful reunion, and life would be normal again.

Life was definitely not normal since his 'aunt' had flown in, under her own wings, uninvited, to live with him. She was, she said, his Guardian Angel, but she was unlike any Guardian Angel he could have imagined. Life had become odd—very odd, and very unsettling.

Piccolo had loved nothing better than to sit by his fish pond and talk softly to the perch, or sort his stamps or read the newspaper. Annabelle would rather dance on a hornets' nest, or wrestle with pirates, hollering happily all the while. She was messy and loud and caused him great embarrassment.

And now Great-Aunt Annabelle had a new hobby. She had been entering all sorts of competitions, raffles, and lotteries, everything from guessing the number of jelly beans in a glass jar to Super Stupendo Lotto. And she was winning nearly every time! It was all terribly annoying for Piccolo. Delivery vans came and went all day, robbers twice a week, then the police would come and plod around grumpily. Piccolo's fine old house had become an obstacle course of

Piccolo's fine old house had become an obstacle course.

prizes. It was taking him twelve minutes just to get from the stairs to the kitchen. Crates of edible things were stacked to the kitchen ceiling. The lounge room was so full of televisions that they had to stand up to watch one. The safe in the cellar was stuffed to bursting with gold nuggets, bars, and coins, and a wide assortment of precious prize jewels, but the thieves had not found their wicked way in there, yet.

There were other things, important things, for Piccolo to be worrying about. Homework, for instance. Every time he sat to make a start, Annabelle would burst into the room crying out something like 'We've won a weekend in Iceland!' or 'Do we have room for a giraffe?'

And there was Annabelle's training to be getting on with. Her next Inspection was just a month away. She was only Piccolo's temporary Guardian Angel—to be able to stay she needed to pass regular Inspections. Every few days Piccolo would try to get her started on her training.

'Annabelle,' he would say in his best organizing voice, 'here's a copy of your timetable, in case you've lost the last *seven* I gave you. *Please* read it and . . .' The bell on the front gate would ring.

'It looks a lovely timetable, Piccolo, but I'd best see who that is. Might be something important!' She would bounce outside to gleefully receive her latest prize.

Annabelle was in the back garden now, hiding her last remaining garden gnome in the vegetable patch, amongst the brussels sprouts.

'The robbers will never look here. Nobody likes brussels sprouts, except you, of course, my exceptional boy.'

'Hmmm,' Piccolo agreed. He had found a broken window at the back of the house.

'They must have got in here.' He supposed the police should be called, again, but they had lost interest in the Grande place and Piccolo didn't really want the thieves to be caught. They were like removal men, reducing the clutter and making more living space.

Annabelle didn't mind much either. She was not a greedy person. Her pleasure was in the actual winning not the collecting, and there was a big world out there full of things still to be won.

For a while Piccolo had marvelled at her good fortune. But now, along with all the interruptions and the overcrowding, there were the rumours and suspicions. Some of the citizens of Clearwater Bay were whispering. Mostly it came from grumpy folk who had never won a single thing in their long unlucky lives.

A particular newspaper woman, Ms Erica Stringer, was always poking her pointy nose into their business. She would appear behind them at the supermarket checkout, or two tables away at the Sunflower Café. Piccolo was sure he saw her scurrying away from their garbage bin one night. This bothered Piccolo enormously. He hated being stalked and talked about, but Annabelle would just say, 'The poor skinny thing is just doing her job, dear.'

Annabelle's extraordinary luck had won her a visit from a special anti-fraud police unit. They strongly suspected she was cheating somehow. Fingers were printed, sniffer dogs sniffed, a lie detector detected (nothing), a police accountant accounted. A doughnut machine was labelled and taken away as evidence. After four days they gave up, packed their van and drove away, annoyed and very disappointed. Piccolo and Annabelle stood on the driveway and waved them off.

'I'm going to miss all those nice young people,' she sighed. 'You don't think I'm a cheat, do you, Piccolo?'

'Of course not,' said Piccolo. Annabelle might be noisy and chaotic but she was too honest and open to cheat. Besides, he knew it was strictly against Angel Law for angels to use their powers for profit or popularity.

But the local Inspector of Guardian Angels was not so sure of her innocence.

One afternoon Piccolo was upstairs hurrying through his maths homework before the next distraction. Annabelle was busy with entries and envelopes, licking and sticking at the kitchen table. From their different ends of the house they heard the regular afternoon crunch of gravel on the driveway.

'Half past four! Surprise time!' She bobbed up from the table like a cork, calling up to Piccolo as she bustled to the front door. 'We might need you to help unload, Piccolo. I'm feeling extra lucky today.'

He sighed, and left his long divisions half divided.

The familiar red postal van idled by the driveway fountain, but an unfamiliar driver was opening its back door.

'Your extraordinary good fortune continues, Miss Grande,' said the new postman. Piccolo recognized him immediately. It was the Inspector. He was a short, stout, humourless man with a snappy thin moustache and a talent for poor disguises.

'Yes, I am a lucky bunny, aren't I?' Annabelle agreed uncomfortably. She recognized him too. Her Inspector, in any of his various costumes, made her very nervous. She and Piccolo had known him previously as a pest exterminator and a pizza shop owner.

'I am Mr Plowright,' he said shaking their hands stiffly. Piccolo and Annabelle introduced themselves as if he were a totally new and interesting person. Piccolo helped him unload the prizes. Today it was cartons of Hungarian pretzels and a Super-Safe home security system. When it was all stacked on the front steps, Mr Plowright presented Annabelle with a pen and a document to sign. Along with Date, Address, and Signature, she read a stiff hand-written note that said:

'The person you see before you is your Inspector.'

As usual, the Inspector badly overestimated the cleverness of his new disguise.

'I will be your postman from now on,' he announced with his artificial smile. He fixed a cold and significant stare on Annabelle and continued. 'So I will be here often, I expect, due to your *supernatural* luck. Ha ha.' His laugh sounded like a painful cough.

'Oh, hah, hah, hah,' winced Annabelle. 'It's all just plain old dumb human luck, I can assure you.'

Mr Plowright coughed his laugh again and retrieved his pen.

'Oh,' he said, 'and this is for you, Master Grande.' He handed Piccolo a postcard. Piccolo put it in his pocket, as the postman put out his hand.

'Good day,' he said, staring through his heavy rimmed glasses as they shook hands again. 'It's been a pleasure to meet you.'

Piccolo struggled to look natural and innocent, and as if the pleasure was his, too. This new postman must not suspect that Piccolo knew his real identity. That was part of Piccolo's great secret.

It was actually a set of secrets. Piccolo was not supposed to know that Annabelle was an angel, or that the Inspector was one too. But the really big secret was a peculiar one.

According to Annabelle, her ordinary, well-organized little boy was an Angelspotter. This is a rare kind of child that can identify angels, even when they are fully disguised, even in the distance, in poor light, in a great crowd of humans. An Angelspotter can see a golden glow around them.

Annabelle had warned her boy to guard these secrets well at all times, especially around Angel Authorities. Mr Plowright, postman and Inspector, was an Angel Authority. If Piccolo's big secret was discovered he would be taken to a special school for Angelspotters. This was a most unhappy place, Annabelle assured him.

At first Piccolo had found all this hard to believe. If he was an Angelspotter he was a very bad one, because he had never seen anybody with a golden glow. He could not tell an angel from a bright green lamppost.

But not long ago he had seen *something* strange; strange enough for him to take Annabelle's warnings seriously; something he did not care to remember. He had seen an A–RF: an Angel—Recently Fallen. Her name was Elspeth, a glorious creature with long flaxen hair, who had enchanted Piccolo. But later Piccolo had seen her true self; a dark and unhappy being, as cold as ice.

The red van drove away at last.

'Phew,' breathed Annabelle. 'He seems very, um, efficient. And familiar?' she wondered, looking quizzically at Piccolo.

'It was the Inspector, of course. A blind mole-rat could see through that disguise,' said Piccolo. 'And you can help unload your prizes from now on. I always think he knows I know, the way he stares at me through those glasses.'

He remembered the postcard in his pocket and fished it out. On it was a photograph of a dog lying on a beach towel, wearing a loud flowery shirt and sunglasses.

'Who's it from?' said Annabelle bouncing next to him. 'Who's it from?'

'It's from Stella,' he read. Stella was a school friend and a favourite of Piccolo's. 'She's in Tahiti for the holidays, having a wonderful time, misses me,' he added, blushing a little. Stella could make him blush very easily, even from as far away as Tahiti.

'She deserves a wonderful time,' said Annabelle.

Stella had played a big part in bringing the unhappy adventure with Elspeth to a happy end. The Angel Authorities had made sure Stella had no memory of the strange events, but Piccolo agreed that she should be rewarded. She had been truly heroic.

'She says it's hot and the pineapples are exceptional.' Piccolo realized he missed her a bit too, and blushed some more.

CHAPTER TWO
A Serious Talk

'Annabelle. We need to have a serious talk. Your prize goats . . .'

Annabelle sat on the kitchen floor almost buried in tin cans, stripping the labels off. She would post them away and win something wonderful. She could feel it.

'Random and Chaos, my precious babies? What about them?'

'No, they are *not* precious.' Piccolo was grinding his teeth. 'They've ring-barked the orange trees, they've trampled the roses, *and*,'

Piccolo paused dramatically, 'they've pooped in the perch pond!'

'Oh dear,' murmured Annabelle, quite seriously. 'In your perch pond. That's awful, Piccolo. I am sorry.'

The perch pond was his special place, his sanctuary, where he went when he was troubled or needed to think. It was not a place to joke about.

'Why don't we build them a pen, or win a tin garage to put them in . . . ?' Annabelle began brightly, but Piccolo was firm, and insisted that they had to go.

'It's not just the goats, Annabelle. There is too much of everything. We have a crisis of stuff. I'm stubbing my toes all the time. I'm sick of it all. Either it all goes or I do.'

'But where will you go, dear?' she chuckled. 'Sorry, sorry. I'm serious now. What can we do?'

'First, I will write a list,' said the orderly boy. He sat down, sharpened a pencil to a needle point and felt better immediately. He was taking control.

The list had three columns with the headings: 'Give Away', 'Sell', 'Bank'. He added a 'Day' column down the side:

Day One—Cash, Jewellery, Gold (These were divided between 'Give Away' and 'Bank'.)

Day Two—Big Ornaments, Bird Baths, Garden Gnomes (He added goats to both the 'Give Away' and 'Sell' columns)

Day Three—Electrical Equipment

And so on.

'Tomorrow can be Day One,' he said firmly. They spent the evening like successful pirates, counting and dividing and piling cash, gems, jewellery, and gold on the kitchen table. Piccolo wrote a 'Goats for Sale' advertisement for the local newspaper, the *Clearwater Klaxon*. He gave them safer names—Bert and Syd—and described them as playful and loving, which was mostly true.

It was getting late. Annabelle looked a little weary and downcast, but Piccolo looked at their labours with satisfaction. His sharp eye paused

They spent the evening like successful pirates.

at the jewellery pile. It looked a little lighter than before.

'Annabelle, are you hiding things in your hair?'

She sheepishly extracted a ring, a bracelet, and three necklaces out of her tangled mass. Piccolo asked her to give her head a shake, and out flew a pair of earrings, a large gold nugget, and a red ballpoint pen that had been missing for a month.

The next morning they stood outside the Dependable Bank, several heavy bags at their feet. Annabelle would not go in.

'No, really, Piccolo, it's not that I want to keep any of it. It's Mr Tompkins, the new manager. He gives me the willies—serious chilly willies.'

Piccolo knew what she meant. There was definitely something creepy about Mr Tompkins. He was very polite and attentive. He would always leap, grinning, out of his office to greet them the second they set foot in the door, and shake their hands too hard and too long.

'He pretends to be friendly,' said Piccolo, 'because he thinks my parents are dead and all their fortune is mine.'

'Creepy and sly and icky,' said Annabelle.

Piccolo agreed to go in alone while Annabelle took the give-away bags to the charity shop. They would meet there in half an hour, then have morning tea at the Sunflower Café.

Piccolo picked up his bags, took a deep breath, and climbed the steps to the bank. Three seconds inside and Mr Tompkins was grinning into his face. The manager's teeth glinted but his eyes were cold. Crushing Piccolo's hand, he led him into his office.

The cold eyes lit up when Piccolo opened up Annabelle's precious parcels on the office desk. Gleaming nuggets and dazzling jewels lit the room.

'My goodness, Master Grande! What a bounty!' he exclaimed, much too loudly. Several staff hurried like greedy bees to a bucket of free nectar and wedged themselves into the doorway. They gasped, oohed, and ahhed.

Curious customers joined them, pressing their faces against the glass wall. They oohed too and jostled each other for a better view. Ms Erica Stringer, the pointy-nosed journalist, was among them scribbling down notes. Piccolo felt extremely uncomfortable.

'All this belongs to my Great-Aunt Annabelle, Mr Tompkins,' he explained. 'She's been lucky, a lot, lately.'

Someone whispered loudly, 'She's been a lucky *crook*, or I'm a tuna sandwich.'

Piccolo glanced over his shoulder to identify the whisperer. He was shocked to see dozens of Clearwater Bay's citizens peering past him at the precious pile. At least one dozen of them were blazered bankers. They all had the same glassy eyes and greedy grin as the manager.

'You have a lot of people working here today, Mr Tompkins,' Piccolo commented.

'What?' said Mr Tompkins absently as he pawed through the jewellery. 'Oh, them, yes. We're having a Dependable Bank District Get-together today,' he explained. 'Very exciting. Banking games, barbecue . . . Oh, look at this one! A ruby, isn't it? About forty carats?' He held up a brilliant red stone. Piccolo had no idea what it was, but thought it looked more like a strawberry than a carrot.

At last all the depositing and signing was done. The crowd had drifted away, sighing, and wondering if they should begin lives of crime. At the door of his office, Mr Tompkins gripped Piccolo's hand again with unfriendly force.

'A pleasure doing business with a Grande, as always,' he grinned as he shook.

Outside there was a murmuring sound, which slowly became a great rumble. Mr Tompkins's hand went clammy and limp, and Piccolo thought he suddenly looked green.

'Well, must go,' he mumbled. 'Business, banking to do . . .' and scurried to his office and shut the door firmly.

Odd, thought Piccolo, as he stepped out into the sunshine, much relieved. The rumbling had passed by. He wondered for a moment what had made the noise and fumes, then set out to meet Annabelle.

She was not at the charity shop as arranged, but this was no surprise. His great-aunt was famously unreliable. The staff at the Sunflower Café had not seen her either. After a grumpy hour or so looking in the rest of the town's charity shops and cafés, Piccolo caught the bus home.

'She'll be all right,' he told himself. But with Annabelle, he could never be too sure.

Later that afternoon, Piccolo was in the back garden, wrestling a birdbath into a wheelbarrow. It was for tomorrow's give-away. Annabelle was still missing. A vehicle crunched its way down the long gravel driveway.

'That will be her at last, in handcuffs in a police car probably,' he guessed. This had happened before. But the gravel crunching sound went on too long, and the horn that tooted was too tinny. There was whooping as well. Even Annabelle would be shy about whooping in a police car—maybe. He trotted nervously to the front of the house.

'Piccolo! Look! I won it!' Annabelle shouted joyfully. She was riding a motor scooter, with a sidecar attached, round and round the driveway fountain. Everything was a startling lolly pink and plastered with yellow daisies; scooter, sidecar, and rotund rider. She skidded to a stop by Piccolo. He stood gaping.

'I won it!' Annabelle repeated, beaming. 'Isn't she beautiful! I've called her Pootles and the sidecar is Little Toot. And look!' She spun round on the seat. The back of her jacket read 'Heaven's Angels'.

'I had it embroidered. Pretty funny, don't you think?'

Piccolo didn't know what to think.

'I know it's more stuff, Piccolo, but she's just so gorgeous! I was in the mall. I passed by an instant draw thingy, and I had two dollars left, and blow me over, what do you know—I won!'

'But you can't drive! You haven't even got a licence!' said Piccolo at last, exasperated.

'Of course I can drive! I drove here, didn't I? Let's go for a ride.'

Piccolo should have said 'No! No way in the world!' and he should have repeated 'You cannot ride without a licence. It is dangerous and illegal!' But Annabelle was so excited, and promised never to win anything else ever, and it was only going to be a tiny drive to the end of their ever-so-quiet street. Piccolo found himself sitting in Little Toot wearing a polo helmet with swimming goggles to protect his eyes. He felt very silly and anxious. Things were slipping out of his control again.

'Are you comfy, dear?' shouted Annabelle, a bit deaf inside her helmet. She took Piccolo's stiff silence for a wholehearted 'yes', yelled 'Yeeehah!' and took off down the driveway.

CHAPTER THREE
On the Road

Near the end of their silent street, Annabelle shouted above Pootles's little BBBRRRIIIIMMM.

'I'll just drive by Mrs Jolly's house. Give her a thrill.'

'No, Annabelle! You said you'd . . .' Cough cough, Piccolo choked on an insect.

'Can't hear you, dear, through this helmet. Oh, good! There she is!'

Mrs Jolly was Pleasant Crescent's most dedicated neighbourhood watcher, and she disapproved of nearly everything, including strangers and unfamiliar vehicles. She was watering her driveway as usual when Annabelle zipped by on the wrong side of the road.

'Yelp,' she cried, and dropped her hose to make an entry in her notebook. Annabelle was then suddenly inspired to give Mr Popolous at the service station a thrill too. 'It's only round the corner, then we'll go home,' she shouted.

Mr Popolous was more alarmed than thrilled as they BBBRRRIIIIMMMed past and he stood, mouth open, pumping petrol onto his shoes. Annabelle intended to take the next corner home, but she was chuckling hard and misjudged the bend. There was a short but eventful trip through the Mayberrys' steep back garden. They clattered across the railway line, then suddenly with a bump they found themselves on Business Drive. This was a serious and busy road which had no time for nonsense. The traffic was not amused by a dazzling pink motor scooter appearing from nowhere. A big truck honked at them. Annabelle, startled, waved back, veering to the centre lane where they were tooted again. A stern little man in a postal van travelling in the opposite direction stared meaningfully at them, and shook his head.

Annabelle concentrated hard on driving in a straight line. Pootles struggled to keep up with the traffic. Annabelle's hair whipped Piccolo about the face and his nose was running with the

cold. It was a miserable and frightening experience. He looked about hopefully for a traffic policeman. It was time to be arrested. But there was no rescue. Pootles and Little Toot, Annabelle and Piccolo were swept by the traffic far away from their quiet Pleasant Crescent.

At last Piccolo spotted an exit ahead and poked Annabelle to get her attention. She understood in the nick of time and swerved suddenly off Business Drive. They puttered to a stop under a friendly looking tree.

'Wow!' she puffed. 'That *was* exciting!'

Piccolo could not unlock his hands from the rim of the sidecar.

'I haven't got a clue where we are. Have you, dear?'

Piccolo looked about. They were near the coast, south of Clearwater Bay. There were a few holiday cottages about, locked up for the winter.

'I think there's a store down the road. My parents used to bring me here for holidays. We'll ring for a tow truck to take us home,' said Piccolo, shaken but sensible. His driver looked disappointed.

'We can*not* go home along Business Drive, Annabelle.'

'What if we wait until dark? We could sneak home . . .'

Piccolo shook his polo-helmeted head, and that was that.

They rode slowly along the beach road. Piccolo had remembered correctly, and they pulled up at the general store.

'That scooter's a beauty,' said the store man. 'Not nuts about the colours, but I bet she runs like a frightened chicken. Puttini 250? With the triple slip diff? And Bertolli suspension? And the Pavorotti sidecar . . . ?' Piccolo left them talking scooters. There was a directory inside the phone box. He looked up tow truck businesses, chose

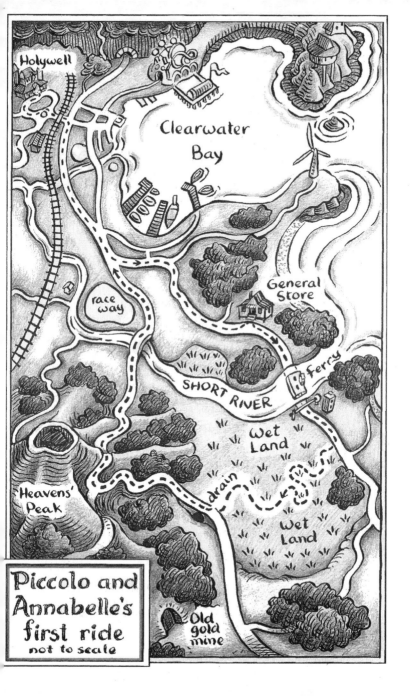

one and dialled. The phone took his money, twice.

Greg, the store man, agreed that the phone was crook. A bored youth had squirted glue into it. Sadly, he explained, the shop phone was crook too, struck by lightning, but there was another on the far side of the ferry.

'Can I sell you anything before you take off?'

Piccolo bought a map. Annabelle bought hot tea, cold drinks, several kinds of elderly sandwiches and a hand of bananas from Brazil. She had a picnic in mind, to pass the time while they waited for a tow truck.

It was a few kilometres further on to the ferry. Piccolo studied his flapping map while his driver sang loudly and merrily.

The ferry sat empty and peaceful on their side of an inlet. They could see a phone box across the water.

Good, thought Piccolo. We're still heading in the wrong direction, but it's worth crossing over, if the phone works.

The ferry driver was pretty sure it did. They pootled up to the front of the ferry and settled down to wait. Annabelle sipped her tea and hummed tunelessly to herself.

'What a glorious day,' she observed.

Piccolo had learned what he could from his new map. He folded it carefully and began his sandwich. It was peaceful by the water. He enjoyed the salty breeze and the soft murmur of the ferry engine. Despite all the drama of the last hour he began to doze lightly in the sunlight. He half dreamt that he could hear a low growling, like distant thunder. The growling grew louder and louder, then suddenly it turned a corner and became a throbbing roar. Piccolo stirred from his nap as two dozen motorbikes trundled onto the ferry. It sank low into the water. The little pink scooter and sidecar were boxed in by the huge thrumming, burbling machines.

Piccolo slid as low as he could into Little Toot

and sneaked a peek sideways. They were surrounded by a sea of beards, black studded leather, and gleaming chrome. He read 'Stinky Cheese Gypsies' on the back of a jacket. There was a dog on the bike closest to him. Piccolo recognized it. It was the scruffy little bus stop dog that lived in town under benches of bus stops. He was now wearing a tiny helmet and goggles. Piccolo was too frightened to think 'Oh, cute'. The ferry ground its way off the shore. It wallowed under the great weight, struggling towards the far side. Piccolo looked up at Annabelle. He was amazed to see that she was completely calm. He had to admire her courage as he huddled, quaking, in Little Toot.

The southern shore drew near. Annabelle started up Pootles, and began to rev her little engine. 'BRRRIM, BRRRRIM, BRRRRIM.'

No, No, No! Don't do that! thought Piccolo desperately. Sure enough, the giant bikes immediately answered Pootles's call.

They were surrounded by a sea of beards.

There was a deafening crescendo of BRRR-RROM, BRRRRROMs.

'BRRRRIM, BRRRRIM,' Pootles replied.

This conversation went on, to and fro. The ferry man steered his craft ashore, opened the gates and sprinted to lift the boom gate that blocked the road ahead. He was keen to see the back of the Stinky Cheese Gypsies.

BRRRRROM BRRRRROM! BRRRRIM, BRRRRIM!

Suddenly Annabelle accelerated, shouting 'Duck!' as they sped off under the half open boom, leaving the big bikes behind. Piccolo noted the phone box as they flashed by. They had a small head start but the pack of bikes was gaining rapidly. Piccolo's heart was pounding. It was crazy and hopeless trying to escape. He looked over at Annabelle, expecting to see grim determination, fighting to save her boy against all odds. But she was grinning like a maniac from ear to pink ear.

They nearly rolled over as Annabelle made a

hard right off the road and along a bumpy track, racing along through muddy scrub. He heard the bikes roar past, stop and grumble, looking for their vanished prey. Annabelle and Piccolo lost precious moments pushing their way through a deep bog. Then they whipped through a tea-tree forest, ducking and weaving. Annabelle slowed down trying to find a clearer track. Piccolo strained to hear the big bikes. They must have given up at the bog, he thought. Annabelle chose a path which led them to a steep road embankment. There was nowhere to go but up. They pushed and pulled, grunting and straining on the loose rocks. Halfway up they stopped to catch their breath, and heard the bikes rumbling towards them along the road. Piccolo had spotted a big drain in the embankment. They scrambled and slid with Pootles back down the slope and squeezed into the drain, just in time. The pack rumbled by slowly overhead. Piccolo blew a huge sigh, and slumped against Little

Toot, exhausted. To his horror the pack rumbled back again and stopped right above them. They stood frozen, listening. A deep voice said, 'Find 'em, Busstop.' There was a sharp scrabbling noise as stones fell, then a small thud. The scruffy dog had landed at the end of their drain. He looked straight at them.

'Good boy,' Annabelle whispered, and added, 'Yip, yip, woof, harf, harf.' Piccolo thought he saw the dog wink before it scrabbled away. He held his breath, waiting for big leathery men to appear. But nothing happened. The bikes trundled away.

CHAPTER FOUR
Up Close and Personal with the Stinky Cheese Gypsies

Annabelle laughed and laughed.

'Whoo, that was a close call! Are you all right, dear? You look a bit pale. Have a banana.'

'That was the bus stop dog. What is he doing with them? And why didn't he bark? Did I see him *wink* at you?' Piccolo was weary and confused, and not in the mood for fruit.

'He must have felt sorry for us, I suppose. How about a nice cool drink?' She opened a can, which had been jostled on its journey, and sprayed everywhere.

'Oops! Sorry, dear. Hah, Hah! What a day we're having!'

Piccolo, confused, weary and now sticky as well, shook the drink off his map. He needed to know where they were, exactly.

'Don't worry about the map, dear. I'll just, you know, take a look around.'

'You can't fly! What if somebody sees you?'

'I'll be careful,' said Annabelle as she took off her Heaven's Angels jacket and stretched her wings. She tiptoed out of the drain with exaggerated caution, looked about dramatically then flapped skywards.

She is having much too good a time, thought Piccolo grumpily. He picked at a damp sandwich. It seemed like a month since he had been sorting jewellery on the kitchen table.

Some ten minutes later Annabelle returned with an untidy thump. She pulled a branch out of her hair.

'Sorry I was so long, dear. Bit of a fight with a tree,' she said, puffing as she put on her jacket. 'North we go, along this road, then over a hill and we're practically home. No sign of the big bikes, or any traffic at all.'

They wrestled their machine up to the road, and set off towards Annabelle's 'hill'. It looked like a Himalayan mountain to Piccolo. Brave little Pootles struggled and very nearly made it to the top before she spluttered to a stop, exhausted.

Annabelle plopped herself down on the flowery roadside.

'Someone will come along. Try to relax,' she said and started a daisy chain. But Piccolo could not relax.

'What if *they* come along?' He was not feeling brave today, especially compared to Annabelle.

'Then we'll hide again.'

'Well I'm hiding now,' he huffed, leaving the road and climbing up into the bush.

Piccolo was actually taking the chance to relieve himself. As he pushed his way through the bush, he began to wonder how long he could survive out here, all alone. A cave or a hollow tree trunk would have to be found. It would be getting cold soon, and a fire would be necessary. He wondered if there were any matches in the sidecar. There were bananas, but when they were gone he would have to forage for roots and berries. Some flowers could be eaten too. He'd had them in salads and he wondered if the ones at his feet were edible. As he bent over and picked some he felt a low rumbling. A sound followed, then faded then grew louder again.

'It's them! They're coming up the mountain!' He ran downhill towards the road, leaping over rocks and branches, his thoughts racing ahead of him. 'We'll push the scooter off the road—hide in the bush. But she's too pink. They'll see her. She can fly off—get help. Home soon, safe and sound. Where's the road?'

Piccolo tripped, tumbled, and landed with a thud. He had found the road. There were black boots and tyres where Annabelle should have been.

'Look who's dropped in! Aw, how nice. He's brought us flowers!' Laughter rumbled all about him. He lay paralysed, his chest hammering, clutching a ragged bunch of salad flowers. Suddenly he found himself jumping up and running straight at a wall of heavy leathery legs. Apparently his plan was to bowl them all over and run to freedom.

'Not so fast, l'il fella,' said a leathery giant as he plucked Piccolo into the air.

A high voice, a woman's voice, chirped, 'That's my boy!'

A familiar pink shape pushed her way through the road block. Piccolo was lowered gently.

He plucked Piccolo into the air.

'Everyone, this is Piccolo. I'm his *Great-Aunt Annabelle*,' she said. Heavy thuds of greeting landed on Piccolo's back. Great hairy paws took his hand. Introductions were made—Dave, the biggest of a very big bunch, seemed to be the leader. Then there was Bruiser, Pongo, Slippery, Nailgun, Slab . . . Piccolo almost wept with relief. He realized that he wasn't going to die after all.

'Poor Pootles isn't well. These gentlemen have offered to fix her,' said Annabelle.

Good, thought Piccolo. Then we can go home.

'So I've invited them home to have a good look at her. Is that all right, dear?'

A host of squinty, bloodshot eyes bored into him. They waited politely for Piccolo's permission to come and destroy his beautiful home. He was appalled, horrified, and aghast, but without a real choice. He squeaked a 'yes'.

They said 'Beaut, Bottler, Onya, Grouse,' and other meaningless grunts, and rumbled into action. Dave gave Annabelle a spare Gypsy helmet. Slippery, who looked as if he'd washed in a bucket of sump oil, loomed over Piccolo. 'Here, mate. I don't like the look of that thing on your head. Have your auntie's hat.' Piccolo obediently took off his polo helmet, which Slippery drop-kicked into the bushes, and put on his aunt's brilliant pink one.

'Very nice,' Slippery chuckled into his beard.

Annabelle climbed up onto a bike behind Dave. Piccolo was lifted into Little Toot. The bus stop dog was plopped on top of him.

'And mustn't forget these,' said Slippery, handing him the crushed salad posy. Pootles, Little Toot, Piccolo, and the dog were attached by a chain behind a massive bike. It had quadruple exhausts. As they thundered over the mountain Piccolo tried not to breathe. The dog on his lap chewed his fleas busily.

'I'm not happy. I'm not happy at all!' he yelled soundlessly into the roar and the fumes. The scruffy dog stopped chewing, concerned, and gave him a sympathetic lick, which caught Piccolo right on the mouth.

CHAPTER FIVE
The Stinky Cheese Picnic

Annabelle and Dave seemed to get along famously. All the way home they shouted to each other and laughed merrily. The big pack of bikes burbled into Clearwater Bay. Townsfolk stepped away, curtains were drawn and windows locked. Shopkeepers closed up early. The blue-blazered bank clerks stared suspiciously from behind their counters. Inside the police station, police officers glanced at each other nervously then went on filling in their paperwork. One of them quietly pulled the phone plug out of the wall.

The pack turned like a swarm of giant black beetles into Piccolo's quiet and leafy crescent. Mrs Jolly on the corner dropped her hose, dived behind a bush, and scribbled in her watch book. Twenty-five heavy bikes, and poor sick Pootles, rumbled down Piccolo's long gravel driveway. The driveway had never seen anything like it.

The Gypsies parked under the olive trees and on the wide circle around the fountain. They dismounted, stretched, scratched, and looked about. The bus stop dog leapt out of Little Toot. Piccolo struggled after him, took off Annabelle's helmet, and coughed up exhaust gas. He took a deep cleansing breath of garden air. But the scent of grass and olive trees was mixed with oily leather and an odour like unwashed feet. A grubby ground sheet was being spread out on the verandah. Piccolo quickly moved his potted palms out of harm's way. Pootles was separated from Little Toot, and plonked down on the ground sheet. Leadpipe and Boof set to her with a variety of tools. Piccolo and Annabelle watched as the little scooter was skilfully turned into a pile of Pootle pieces.

'Don't worry, miss. She'll be right,' Leadpipe assured Annabelle.

'You've slipped ya cleat clean off ya diff,' explained Boof, 'an' it could take a while to find annuver one.'

Piccolo asked nervously how long a while.

'Aw, geez . . . round these parts . . . waddaya reck'n, Leadpipe?' who tugged at his oily beard. 'Coupl'a days, if we're lucky.'

Piccolo's heart sank. Surely they did not need twenty-five bikers to stay forty-eight hours to fix one tiny Pootles! He looked pleadingly at Annabelle, but she seemed unconcerned, even pleased.

'Good! Then you'll need to call some scooter people? There's a phone in the hall,' she said brightly. Piccolo watched in dismay as Boof and

Leadpipe walked their great knobbly boots onto his beautiful polished floor. Annabelle invited Dave in for a cup of tea. Piccolo turned the kettle on and put out some biscuits. He hoped the big bearded man would like dainty cream wafers. He and Annabelle chatted and teased in such a familiar way that Piccolo asked 'Do you two already know each other?'

Annabelle said they did indeed. She and Dave were old friends. Piccolo wondered about this, because he knew that Annabelle had been in an African jungle the last two hundred years. She had been Guardian Angel to a troop of chimpanzees right up until she came to stay with him.

'So you met in the jungle?'

'That's right,' said Annabelle. 'I was there, ah, studying chimpanzees; Dave was an explorer, weren't you, Dave, exploring my jungle?'

'That's right,' Dave agreed, slowly. 'Before I was a Gypsy I was looking for, um, diamonds.

Found this little jewel, too. Har, Har.' He gave Annabelle a squeeze around the middle, and she blushed furiously.

'So, you recognized each other on the mountain today?'

Annabelle confessed that she had known it was Dave straightaway on the ferry. The entire hair-raising chase and escape had been a game for them.

'Sorry, Piccolo, I should have said. I got a bit carried away. It was fun though, yes?'

Being a truthful boy, he wanted to say 'No, I was terrified the whole time,' but he said 'Yes. Very exciting. Thank you.' He did not want Dave thinking he was a nervous Nellie.

The scooter fixing, now postponed, became a picnic—a noisy, cheesy picnic. The gang was called Stinky Cheese Gypsies for a reason. Out of leathery pockets and saddle bags came cheeses: stinky ones, squashed and pungent; green cheese, blue cheese, cheese full of veins. The fumes drifting into the kitchen made Piccolo's eyes water. Out came crackers, too, and sour milk to wash it all down. They spread themselves out on the lawns and verandahs, munching and mumbling. Now and then there were huge eruptions of laughter, followed by quieter periods of serious cheese eating. Slippery brought Piccolo a selection of his personal favourites, balanced on an oily saddle bag. Piccolo said he would be sure to try them all, later, and thank you so much. He thought he saw crawling things inside the cheeses.

Gradually the picnic turned into a party. The cheese was making some of them light-headed. There was silliness and increasing rowdiness. Suddenly two of them jumped on their bikes, apparently to go out for more cheese.

'And get us some Roquefort, Extra Old—two kilos. Wait. Better make it ten. Good onya, Brick,' shouted Numnut, and off they roared.

As the short winter day faded, the party grew livelier. The Gypsies lit little fires up and down the driveway. They looked very homely, dancing in the chilly evening.

They're probably burning my antique furniture, Piccolo thought helplessly. He would be feeling small and helpless for much of the long night ahead.

Races began along the driveway. Two bikes would start at the front gate and roar towards the house then spin skilfully to a stop by the fountain. Watching from the verandah, Piccolo ducked to avoid great showers of driveway gravel.

The noise of the bikes and the Gypsy cheering was terrific. Piccolo expected to hear sirens approaching any minute. The police, however, had all gone home early to bed.

Random and Chaos, the goats, were discovered and added to the driveway sprints. A goat would be carefully balanced with its front legs over a rider's shoulders. The bike would zoom along then brake suddenly. The goat would sail, bleating happily, through the air, end over end. The rider whose goat flew the furthest was the winner. The goats were caught by a Gypsy, of course. They were a rough bunch, but kind to goats.

In the middle of all this merriment, the cheese-buying Gypsies returned.

They disappeared around the back of the house with great lumpy bundles—enough cheese for a year rather than a Pootles-fixing forty-eight hours, Piccolo thought.

He wondered where Annabelle was, and if she knew what was happening to her goats. He found her in the kitchen, deep in conversation with Dave and the cheese buyers. The bus stop dog, whose name appeared to be Busstop, was on the table. He seemed to be listening intently. Dave was talking low and urgently.

'Take another six blokes with you next time. Split up, then . . .' Busstop spotted Piccolo and yipped. Everyone fell silent and looked over at the boy, alone and little by the door. He felt like an intruder, in his own home.

'Oh hello, dear,' said Annabelle brightly. 'We're just planning another shopping trip. Big cheese eaters, these Gypsies. Are you keeping them sensible out there?'

Piccolo was about to say something about her flying goats when someone boomed cheerily behind him.

'Hey, where's that little fella? There you are,' said Block. 'Come and get a load of this!' Piccolo felt he was not wanted at the kitchen conference and was being removed deliberately. Block, his babysitter, sat him down on the verandah steps.

'This'll get rid of ya grumps, sport,' he chuckled.

The goat races had finished without injury. Two Gypsies with extra large tummies were now sizing each other up near the fountain, growling and

He felt like an intruder, in his own home.

snarling good-naturedly. The audience shouted advice, and bet fine cheeses on who would win. Away in the shadows bikes started up and cruised down the driveway. Why, Piccolo wondered, did eight big men need to go shopping for cheese, again, on a wintery night, and what shops would still be open anyway?

A round of belly bouncing commenced. The two large gents ran full tilt at each other. There was a wobbly smack of leathery bellies colliding. The ancient rules of belly bouncing stated that the Gypsy left standing was the winner. It was all so ridiculous that Piccolo found himself laughing along with the Gypsies. Cheese eating continued all the while. Big people were getting louder and sillier. By the ninth round, queasy with the cheesy fumes, Piccolo decided he had seen enough. Just then, his enormous babysitter stood up.

'Time I showed 'em how it's done properly, little mate,' he growled, slapping his great gut.

Piccolo slipped away upstairs to his room, closed the door and fell on his bed.

Stamps! he thought. I must look at my stamps. He took a selection from his shelves, sat down on his bed and tried to ignore the roaring hubbub outside.

'Ah! The Belgian Empire, Volume One,' he read, feeling better already. Piccolo usually found his stamps very soothing. But he was only on the second page when the roaring moved inside the house.

'No, no, no! They can't come in! Why doesn't Annabelle do something?' He left the Belgian Empire and ran downstairs.

This was too much. It was more than too much. The Gypsies had found the trampoline in the ballroom. They had tromped their big boots and cheese inside, and were trying to bounce bellies mid-air. Piccolo stood at the ballroom door with his hands on his head, horrified. Two big men were bouncing higher and higher.

Suddenly they lunged in mid-air towards each other. They slapped together and ballooned into the arms of their guffawing comrades. Piccolo backed away into the kitchen.

'Yip!' said Busstop when he spotted him. Annabelle and Dave were still sitting close together at the table. Maps were spread out before them.

'How are you going, pet? Is it getting a bit rowdy for you?' asked Annabelle.

Piccolo, speechless, pointed limply towards the ballroom. Dave stood up.

'Sorry, mate. They get a bit excited. I'll clear them out.'

He put his heavy arm around Piccolo and set off to empty the house. As they reached the hall a Gypsy hurried in with 'shopping' news.

'We've got some more, ah, cheeses, Dave,' he mumbled, glancing at Piccolo. 'But there are still some more to, um, buy . . .'

'We'll let these fellows talk cheese business,

love,' said Annabelle. 'Let's see if we can't calm things down. We could show them your stamps, that could work. Hah hah.'

Piccolo was not amused. Giant leathery bottoms on his ottoman were no laughing matter. There were boots on his mother's antique carpets. There were secrets going on. It was all a nightmare.

'OK, boys! That's enough! Out you go! Oh, that looks like fun. Piccolo, can I have a go before they stop . . . ?' But he was gone, on his way to his perch pond. It was one place where he could always find some peace. He hoped the Gypsies had not found it already, and eaten his perch.

CHAPTER SIX
Things That Go Lump in the Night

Piccolo did not reach his sanctuary. As he passed through the orange grove he noticed shadowy movements near a garden shed. He crept silently through the trees. Men were moving 'shopping' bundles. Piccolo had a rush of anger. This was not right, secrets and bundles in the night, in his own back garden. Blossom, the biggest and second ugliest of the gang, was quietly talking to another Gypsy.

'This shed's full, Drainpipe. Try the cellar next.'

'No good. It's chock-a-block.'

In the shadows Piccolo's mind was racing. 'They're thieves or smugglers! Those big bundles can't all be cheese! Is Annabelle part of all this? She has to be! She's definitely Dave's best friend.'

Drainpipe left Blossom to guard the full shed. Piccolo took a deep breath and stepped out of the gloom.

'Hello, Blossom.' The ugly giant jumped a foot in the air, squealing.

'Geez, mate! You scared me half to death!'

'There's another shed further down the garden if you need more space for your shopping,' Piccolo began helpfully. 'Is it all cheese? There sure is a lot of it.'

'Yep, all cheese,' said Blossom gruffly to the tiny, sneaky spy. 'Well, mostly cheese and some cheese crackers, and other cheese products. We buy lots, and then we eats it. Thanks, though, about the extra shed.' Then he folded his great arms and whistled the national anthem at the night sky. Piccolo stood waiting for more conversation, then wandered away. He wished intensely that he was not just a feeble boy. If he was bigger, massively big and muscled, he would flick Blossom aside and look in the shed for himself.

A great commotion erupted at the front of the house. Piccolo was torn between finding peace and quiet at the perch pond and investigating the fresh uproar. He decided on the uproar.

There could be no peace by his pond tonight anyway. He jogged back through the gardens. Bikes had returned with more mystery bundles. These were quickly spirited away. Fresh rich cheeses were being unwrapped, and a parcel of Pootles parts! This was the best news that Piccolo had heard all day. The scooter was reassembled quickly and expertly.

'Where's our little mate? He should 'ave a go on Pootles now she's right.'

'There he is! Hiding in that tree,' bellowed Grim.

Piccolo slunk out from behind his olive tree. Lump, the daintiest of the Gypsies, sat carefully on Pootles. Piccolo was put on his lap and allowed to steer for a few circuits of the fountain and a return trip up the driveway. Lump grunted some quick instructions on clutch and accelerator, then left Piccolo on his own. Unhelpful roars of laughter followed him about as he puttered and stalled, puttered and stalled again.

Concentrating fiercely he was able to stop the stalling and hopping. On his third circuit of the driveway he had Pootles fairly well worked out. He even did a quick tour of the orchards in the back garden.

A dangerous thought came to him as he zigzagged amongst the trees. I could just ride away and leave here! I could pack a bag and sneak out in the middle of the night. Annabelle has her new smuggling business and her old boyfriend back. She doesn't need me to look after her any more.

There was thunderous applause when he pulled up at the front steps. Annabelle stood with Dave, clapping heartily.

When the congratulations and back thumping had died down, Annabelle asked Piccolo if the Gypsies could stay overnight. It was getting late after all.

'Yeah, Ugly needs his beauty sleep.' There were roars of laughter at Ugly's expense. Ugly was famous for being the ugliest of them all, uglier even than Blossom.

'And they'll all be as quiet as mice, won't you, boys?' added Annabelle.

'Too right we will!' they roared.

Piccolo could hardly say 'No, I think you should all go *now*, and take your horrible stinking cheese with you.' Besides, some were already stringing up hammocks. Others were cleaning their teeth in the fountain.

Piccolo said that they could stay.

Lying on his bed he listened to the comings and goings of motorbikes, and the rise and fall of conversations. Most of the big cheesy men were settling down for the night.

At long last Piccolo fell into queasy, uneasy dreams. He tossed and turned, hunted by giants on motorbikes the size of houses, with gigantic round cheeses for wheels. He was escaping down a mountainside, and tumbled onto a ferry which

Piccolo fell into queasy, uneasy dreams.

sailed along an inlet. Annabelle was floating about above him, grinning.

'That way, quickly!' she cried, pointing out to sea. The ferry took him across the waves. A yacht sailed ahead, *Leaping Susan* on its stern.

'My parents!' shouted Piccolo as it disappeared into a thick mysterious mist. 'NOOO— wait! I'm coming to save you!' he called and woke himself up.

He knew he would not get back to sleep. The dangerous thoughts, the ones he had on Pootles as he rode about the garden, grew in his mind.

'I'll do it! I'll get out of here. I'll find my parents!'

He dressed and began collecting things he would need on his journey: a compass, his new map, a backpack. In the kitchen he gathered some food, biscuits mostly, no cheese, and a water bottle.

Annabelle will think I've been kidnapped, thought Piccolo, so he scribbled a quick note, and left it on the kitchen table. Money would be needed, lots of it, to buy a boat and supplies. His heart was hammering as he crept down to the cellar. It all felt like another dream. In a moment Annabelle would pop out from a door and say, 'Good morning, Piccolo. Would you like a big banana brekky?'

Gypsy snoring came up from the cellar. Piccolo groped along in the inky dark, stepping carefully over and around lumpy bundles of 'shopping'. He found the vault, unlocked it, and stuffed wads of cash into his bag, then locked it again. As he tiptoed away there was a huge SNNNORRRRKKFFF. Piccolo tripped and landed on a lumpy bundle. He lay still, holding his breath. The Gypsy snuffled some more and said, 'Gotcha, ya slippery little mmmmnnnnpph-hfff.' Piccolo relaxed, then he noticed that the bundle under him was warm—warm and twitching! He stifled a yelp. This shopping is alive! Piccolo thought. He scrambled out of the cellar, ran up the stairs and out onto the driveway. Piccolo looked back at the house in horror. Could he just run away and leave whatever it was tied up in the cellar? But the snores of the Gypsies all about him were now a dangerous chorus. These were more than just enormous; smelly, noisy boys. They had been stuffing live things in sacks, in secret, at night. He would have to escape.

CHAPTER 7
A Dawn Departure

Pootles was parked by the front steps. Piccolo struggled with the zip of the sidecar cover. He wanted to put his pack in there, but the zip was frosted fast and his fingers soon became numb. Giving up, he put the pack on his back and Annabelle's helmet on his head and began wheeling Pootles along the driveway. The machine seemed heavy, and there was too much gravel noise. He fumbled in the dim light trying to unhook Little Toot and leave it behind. He was becoming panicky. There were sleeping

Gypsies to his left and right strung up between the olive trees.

'No, Mum! I *didn't* eat it,' one of them called out in his sleep. Piccolo froze for a long moment, his heart thumping. The guilty Gypsy said nothing more. Leaving Little Toot attached, he began pushing again. At the front gate he climbed on to Pootles, and let her roll a long way down Pleasant Crescent before he turned the key. Pootles sprang to life. The first rosy streaks

of dawn lit the sky. Exhilarated, he sped away on his adventure. He was going to find his parents.

As Piccolo rode along, his mind sped ahead. He would go south to Porpoise Point and buy a small seagoing motorboat and lots of fuel. The boat people would look after Pootles. He had been taught how to sail on *Leaping Susan*, but a motor-boat would be quicker.

His parents were last seen sailing north. It was an old, cold trail but it was the only starting point Piccolo had. Eventually, he would find their desert island, and Peter and Marjorie Grande would be astonished and delighted to see him. They would have much to talk about as they sailed joyfully home.

'I hope the Gypsies leave some of our home to return to,' he worried. 'And what if they are still there?' But his parents would take care of any problems. It would be wonderful to be a small boy again with sensible parents to care for him.

Clearwater Bay lay behind as he followed the main road south. There was very little traffic and Pootles motored along comfortably. Piccolo made a mental list of provisions he would need to buy at Porpoise Point. 'Sea charts, dried soup, extra socks . . .' A knocking interrupted his listing. Pootles was steering poorly.

'A flat tyre? Do I know how to change a tyre?'

He turned off the road into a rest area. The tyres looked fine. As he poked them with a stick, the side car began rocking and knocking. Piccolo jumped back.

'There's something in there!'

The rocking stopped, then suddenly started again, this time with muffled cries.

I'll have to get it out, whatever it is. It must be suffocating, thought Piccolo.

Clutching his tyre-poking stick in one hand, he approached Little Toot. It could be something toothy, possibly an angry baboon. With his free hand he tugged at the difficult zip until it came free. Piccolo jumped back again, with his stick raised. Nothing emerged. Piccolo looked inside Little Toot. A bundle wriggled vigorously. It was one of the Gypsy's mysterious shopping bags! The contents cried, 'Let me out! I can't breathe!'

This is not a baboon and definitely not cheese, thought Piccolo, who knew a bit about angry baboons after his adventures with Elspeth.

He fumbled with the rope binding. A head popped out, gasping. Piccolo recognized it.

'Mr Tompkins? Is that you?'

Piccolo had been gone for half an hour when a Gypsy stirred. Something was bothering Leadpipe. Too much cheese? Probably. And something else. He scratched himself and picked some blue-green crumbs out of his wiry beard. 'Hmmm, yum.' He blearily looked about the back verandah where half a dozen Gypsies were still snoring and snuffling.

'Blast and bother,' he said, sitting up suddenly. 'I remember now. That bundle's still in the sidecar. Gawd 'elp me!' he muttered, rolling out of his hammock with a thud. 'I hope it hasn't suffocated! Where's Pootles parked at?' He hurried off to look about, thinking, Block moved it last.

He found Block in a hammock strung between two straining olive trees. He poked at him with his boot. Block stirred and woke sourly. He had parked Pootles by the front steps, now shoo!

Leadpipe could see the front steps from where he stood. There was nothing there but gravel and frost-covered cheese wrappings.

After some more boot prodding, then a solid kick, Block got up. He squinted at the front steps and agreed that Pootles was not there. They stood on the empty spot, muttering and tugging their beards. Leadpipe noticed fresh footprints on the frosty gravel, heading away down the

Leadpipe noticed fresh footprints.

drive. Next to them were the double tyre marks of Pootles and Little Toot.

'She went thataway. Maybe Blossom took her for a ride. Those are little footsteps, an' he's got dainty feet . . .'

'Yer, or Annabelle maybe.'

But Blossom was where he should be, snoring on the verandah. They tiptoed in their big boots upstairs to Annabelle's room. She was home too.

'Wake her up, Block.'

'No, you wake her up!' hissed Block.

'I'm awake,' said Annabelle. 'Can't you boys sleep? There's not much room in here, I'm afraid.' They mumbled their short story about missing Pootles.

'Where's Piccolo?' she asked anxiously. The three of them tiptoed in a bulky procession to Piccolo's room. He was missing too. A general alarm was quickly raised, but the bleary Gypsies could find no boy or Pootles. Busstop skittered about trying to pick up Piccolo's scent. He hopped up onto the kitchen table, unfolded a note and appeared to read it. He yipped for attention.

Annabelle read:

Dear Annabelle,

If you find this I have gone to look for my parents. Please mind the house until we get back and don't forget to feed the fish. I'll be all right. Don't follow me. I'll look after Pootles. Be back soon.

Love Piccolo

'Oh that poor, silly boy! It's my fault,' she fretted as she bustled around and around the kitchen table. 'I've been ignoring him, and there's been too much excitement.' More self-ishly she added, 'If my Inspector finds out he's gone, I'll get the sack for sure!'

A council was held around the table. A map of the district was found, laid out, and divided into eighths. Dave split the Gypsies into search parties. Block and Leadpipe shuffled uncomfortably nearby. Block nudged Leadpipe and whispered fiercely 'Tell 'er!' and Block hissed back, 'You tell 'er. You left it in there!'

Annabelle looked up from the map. 'Tell me what, Block? Left what in where?'

'Ah well, miss . . .' He looked at his boots, like a great ugly schoolboy caught chewing gum in class.

'We—Leadpipe an' me that is—we left one of them bundles in your sidecar, just for a minute . . . an' we sort of forgot . . .' he trailed off.

The blood drained from Annabelle's face. 'And Piccolo is riding around with it. Will it wake up?'

'Well, yeah. If it hasn't suffocated. They usually wake up in about a day or so, depending,' Block explained.

'How long ago did you catch it?' asked Dave. His beard bristled angrily.

'Ahh, Let's see. There was them others in town, then the one Blossom got at the fish shop . . . ah, 'bout a day ago, or so,' he concluded.

Annabelle hopped on the spot with worry. Final instructions were given and arrangements made. Burly men rushed about putting on boots and helmets and wheeling out their bikes. There was no time for breakfast or even to brush and floss their teeth. Blossom was told to stay by the telephone. Slippery and Drainpipe would guard the bundles in the cellar and the sheds.

Dave held Annabelle. She was shaking.

'He'll be all right, luv. Even if it wakes up, the thing is tied in a bag and zipped up in Little Toot. And even if it got out it would just take off. That kind aren't interested in ordinary boys.'

Annabelle was about to tell Dave that Piccolo was not an ordinary boy, that he was an Angel-spotter, but she held her tongue. There was too much to explain, and the bikes were roaring outside.

CHAPTER EIGHT
Mr Tompkins of the Dependable Bank

'Mr Tompkins! The bank manager!' Piccolo was amazed. 'The Gypsies are smuggling *bank managers?*'

The little crumpled man blinked and shielded his eyes. 'Please don't hit me!' he squeaked breathlessly. After hours and hours trussed in a bag, Mr Tompkins was half blinded by the sunrise. He could see that his enemy was just a boy, but a boy armed with a sharp tyre-poking stick.

'It's me, Mr Tompkins, Piccolo Grande. I was in your bank yesterday, with jewellery and things.'

'Master Grande? Are you with them, that gang?'

'Gang? The Stinky Cheese Gypsies, you mean?' Piccolo lowered his stick. 'No, of course not.'

'Murderous cut-throat kidnapping thieves they are.' He paused to have an attack of wheezing.

'What are you doing in there, Mr Tompkins?'

'Suffocating mostly,' he gasped, 'and being kidnapped. Are you sure you're not a kidnapper too?'

'No! I'm running away from them. They're all at my place.'

'Very wise to run away,' Mr Tompkins approved. 'Can you help me out, please?'

Standing up at last, Mr Tompkins straightened his blazer and smoothed his hair.

'It's unfortunate that you chose this vehicle to

run away in. Those dim criminals will remember that I was in it. They will hunt us down as I am a witness to their crimes. Would you be so good as to take me to the Dependable Bank, as quickly as possible?' he asked.

Piccolo hesitated. He was supposed to be running away in the other direction. But Mr Tompkins looked so pathetic. His disturbing grin was gone. His cold eyes were clouded with fear.

'Yes, all right. But the bank? Not the police?' Piccolo asked.

'No, the bank if you please. There might be some Dependable staff still hiding there. I'm their manager and must therefore take care of them.'

Piccolo helped Mr Tompkins back down into Little Toot. He started Pootles and turned back towards the centre of town.

'Those stinking brutes were after all of us,' explained Mr Tompkins as they rode along. 'We were having an innocent barbecue together and they just burst in and smashed up my lovely bank and tried to kidnap us all. Some may have escaped.'

The little man's story sounded unbelievable. But there had been strange goings-on last night. Piccolo did not know what to think.

They reached the Dependable Bank. Pootles was hidden in a Dependable garage at the rear of the bank. The Gypsies could be about, hunting.

Piccolo joined Mr Tompkins, searching inside. He needed to see for himself if this incredible tale could be true. The bank was a disaster zone. Signs of struggle were everywhere. Furniture and barbecue were upturned, paper strewn about. There were clumps of feathers scattered about as if the Gypsies had attacked the bankers with pillows. Great wads of money were lying about carelessly, and gold nuggets and jewellery were strewn amongst half-cooked sausages. Robbery was obviously not the motive. As Piccolo picked his way through the chaos he recognized a bracelet of Annabelle's, and her string of black pearls . . . and her favourite garden gnome? What was that doing here?

Mr Tompkins was running about, calling. He looked in the vault, in the toilets, under tables. There was not a Dependable banker to be found.

Piccolo sat on a bag of cash to ponder the

gnome. His foot squelched in something unpleasant; something very odorous. It was a block of squashed cheese: Roquefort, Extra Extremely Old, he guessed. This was undeniable evidence! Mr Tompkins had not been zipped inside Little Toot inside a cheesy bag by some bizarre accident. And the warm, wriggling bundle in the cellar was probably a kidnapped banker too. And all the 'shopping' in the garden shed. Piccolo had been consorting with criminals! He had eaten their food and watched them at play.

'Can Annabelle really be mixed up in all this?' He was desperate to make sense of it all. 'Is she a criminal too? Or maybe she's being duped by the Gypsies?'

There was a familiar rumbling, growing louder.

'It's them!' squealed Mr Tompkins. He leapt for the vault and tried to shut himself in. 'Help me!' he squealed. 'It's jammed!'

Piccolo pulled at debris stuck under the door as Mr Tompkins pushed on it in a panic.

There was a familiar rumbling, growing louder.

Through a window they glimpsed a pack of three bikes cruising down the street. The riders were looking this way and that. They slowed to a crawl as they neared the bank.

'Too late! Quickly! Back to the garage!' hissed Mr Tompkins.

Piccolo, doubled over, scrabbled after him. They opened the garage door and pushed the scooter out as silently as possible. The bikers were inside the bank, turning things over.

'Take me away from here!' hissed Mr Tompkins.

'Where are we going?' whispered Piccolo.

'Flounder Town. There's a Dependable Bank there I can hide in.' Mr Tompkins, looking a bit green, ducked down inside Little Toot and tried to zip himself in.

Piccolo pushed Pootles a block or so along a back lane, then started her up.

The little motor sounded dangerously loud in the quiet of a Sunday morning.

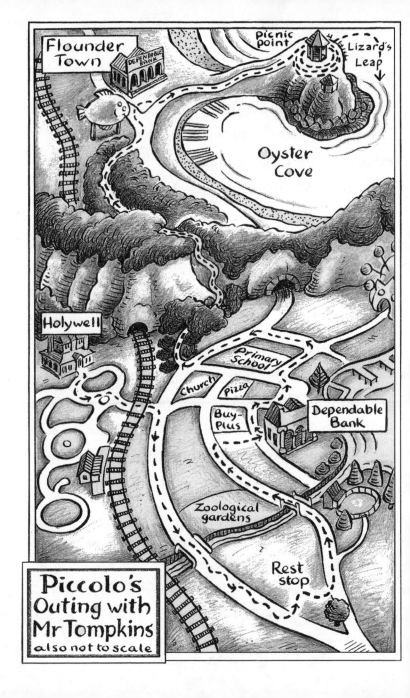

They crept along slowly, keeping to the lanes. For one terrifying moment they saw the black mass of a cruising pack ahead. Reaching the edge of town, Piccolo stopped behind a garden wall to check his map. Mr Tompkins's head popped up.

'What's happening? Why have we stopped?'

'There is a track running over the ridge and behind some scrub nearly all the way to Flounder Town. We'll be harder to spot going that way. Are you all right, Mr Tompkins?' Piccolo noticed that he was looking very green now.

'Yes, yes. Let's be going, Master Grande,' he said testily.

So for the second time in twenty-four hours Piccolo was fleeing along a bumpy dirt track.

CHAPTER NINE
At Lizard's Leap

Annabelle and Dave and two Gypsies stood inside the ruined bank.

'Anybody home?' called Nutburger. There was no reply. 'Service here is terrible,' he said solemnly.

'Oh, here's some of my jewellery,' said Annabelle, stooping and quickly slipping her pearl necklace into her hair, then a couple of nuggets, and some diamond earrings for good luck.

'You blokes could have tidied up a bit,' said Dave.

'They put up quite a fight, boss, and some of the slippery beggars were getting away. Not much time for housekeeping,' said Nutburger defensively.

'We'd better get going, Dave,' said Annabelle. 'They could be miles away by . . . Listen! Did you hear that? It sounded just like my Pootles starting up!'

They ran from the dismantled bank and leapt onto their giant bikes.

Piccolo and his cranky passenger had reached the end of the track. Before them was an exposed stretch of the main road. Flounder Town was only a minute away. They could see the giant fibreglass flounder, the town's main attraction, a few hundred metres along the road.

I'll drop Mr Tompkins off and keep heading north, thought Piccolo. I can't go back through Clearwater Bay to Porpoise Point. There'll be

Gypsies everywhere. I'll buy a boat at Pilchard Reef.

'Go! Let's go! I must get to the bank quickly!' demanded Mr Tompkins. Piccolo peered up and down the road. It was clear. He accelerated out of the bushes towards the town.

'There it is!' cried his agitated passenger, pointing at the Dependable Bank, Flounder Town branch. As they passed by the Giant Flounder, a dog started yapping, loud and long. Piccolo spun around and looked up. There was Busstop on top of the great fibreglass fish. Gypsies were in town! Somewhere, big motors roared.

'Faster! Go faster!' shrieked green Mr Tompkins in Piccolo's ear. But it was too late. A menacing pack turned into the road ahead, blocking their way to the bank.

'Up there! Go up there!' Mr Tompkins shrieked, pointing to a track close to their right.

'But it's a dead end. There's just a lookout on the cliff!' Piccolo objected.

'GO THERE!' screamed Mr Tompkins in a high panic, grabbing the scooter's handlebars and jerking the wheel onto the track.

Piccolo was right. There was nowhere to go except through the safety railing, then a hundred vertical metres to rocks below. Mr Tompkins ordered Piccolo to stop by a picnic shelter. The Gypsies slowly approached up the track. They were trapped. The agitated bank manager leapt out of Little Toot onto a picnic table.

'Stay back!' he screamed.

The Gypsies slowed to a stop. Piccolo wondered why. A small boy and a thin panicky bank manager would not take a lot of overpowering. He looked over at Mr Tompkins, thinking he may have a Dependable Bank hand gun. His mouth dropped open. There was no weapon but Mr Tompkins was transforming before his eyes. The greenish tinge became a bright grass green and horns appeared on his forehead. His cold eyes were now a piercing yellow and rolling wildly.

More Gypsies were arriving on the track below. Mr Tompkins leapt about the picnic shelter. He threw off his blue bank blazer, releasing a pair of black leathery wings.

He pounced on poor astonished Piccolo, pulled him off the scooter, jammed him in the sidecar, zipped him inside and jumped onto Pootles.

'Come any closer and I'll drive this over the cliff!' he screamed at the Gypsies gathering below.

Mr Tompkins ground into gear and wallaby-hopped crazily around and around the picnic shelter. Piccolo struggled with the zip, opening it most of the way. He caught a glimpse of a single bike separating from the others. It chugged slowly up the hill. Someone was calling out.

'Give up, Sariel. Let the boy go.'

Mr Tompkins screamed 'NEVER!' and pointed Pootles at the cliff fence.

'Clear off! All of you, and I'll let this wretch go!'

But the big bike crept closer. It was only fifty metres away now. The Gypsy said, 'You've lost, Sariel. We have all the others. Let the boy go.'

'I'LL SEE YOU ALL IN HELL!' the demon Mr Tompkins screamed and he rode straight at the fence. Piccolo squeezed his eyes shut. He felt a crunch as the fence gave way. His stomach rose into his throat as the machine plummeted. He opened his eyes for an instant, saw Mr Tompkins flapping out to sea, then shut them for the end.

There was a solid jerk. The plummeting stopped. Something very strong had plucked him from Little Toot, and now he floated in its grip.

I've been saved by an eagle, he thought. He was lowered gently onto the rocks at the base of the cliff, not far from the crumpled heap of Pootles and Little Toot. His legs buckled under

There was a solid jerk.

him. White-faced fishermen clutched their rods and stared. They were staring goggle-eyed at something behind Piccolo. He turned to look. There was Dave, smiling, a broad pair of wings folded behind him.

'Dave? You're an angel? I thought you were a kidnapper. Wow, look! There's some more.' Piccolo pointed skywards. A dozen dark feathered shapes were zooming out to sea. A pink round one flapped down from the cliff top. It landed almost on top of him, and smothered him with kisses.

'Oh, thank goodness. Oh, Piccolo. I was so afraid!' She paused in her kissing to grab Dave's legs. 'Thank you, my hero.' Dave beamed down at her.

'No worries, little lady,' he said in a cowboy drawl.

She returned to kissing Piccolo. This time he did not shrink away thinking 'erk'. He welcomed her big pink hug as he began to shake with shock.

'Annabelle! Dave's an angel,' he blurted. 'I thought he was evil, and you too. And Mr Tompkins is a devil or something. I was running away—to find my parents. He turned green and grew horns. I thought he had a gun but . . .'

As Piccolo prattled on excitedly the fishermen packed up hastily and clambered away over the rocks. Dave called out 'Hey! You blokes! How about some cheese?'

'No, mate. We're right,' said a brave one as he dropped his rod and fled. Dave glided ahead of them, cutting off their retreat.

'Aw, come on. I've got a beaut stinky one here,' said friendly Dave. He pulled a knife out of his leather boot. The terrified men cowered in a bunch by a boulder as Dave approached them, carefully taking a cheese from his pocket.

'It's a 1953 Yellow Vein—a classic. You'll love it.' He grinned and cut the cheese.

The clump of fishermen were enveloped in a yellow fog. They slumped onto the rocks and began to snooze peacefully. Dave returned to Annabelle and Piccolo, chuckling.

'That's a powerful fine cheese. Mystifies every time. They won't remember any of this excitement.'

Piccolo laughed too, a little hysterically. He had recently been saved from a rocky end, and was extremely pleased to say the least.

'I thought you'd kidnapped Mr Tompkins for ransom. But what sort of bank manager grows horns?'

'They come in all kinds, mate. Hey, listen. Why don't you have a whiff of this too?' suggested Dave, waving the '53 Yellow Vein under Piccolo's nose.

'That's disgusting, Dave,' he said truthfully, then went on telling his story excitedly.

'We were in the bank—it was a mess—your stuff was everywhere and your gnome, Annabelle —and I saw some Gypsies. Pootles was hidden around the back.' His wits were returning to him, except in one respect. Piccolo failed to realize that Dave was trying to Mystify him.

An Angelspotter cannot be Mystified, so, to protect Piccolo's secret, Annabelle had trained him to pretend to fall asleep should *anyone* spray him with *anything*, even the perfume ladies squirting customers in the department store. Any one of them could be an Angel Authority.

'It could be an Angel trying to Mystify you,' she had explained. They had gone over it again and again. But at the moment, Piccolo was full of the wonder of being saved from certain death and he wasn't being *sprayed* as such.

Dave looked quizzically at Annabelle.

'That cheese could knock out a horse. And what's he doing, seeing demons? What's going on here?'

Annabelle looked pained.

'It's a long story . . .' she shrugged, 'and I kept meaning to tell you but . . .' She stopped as

Flathead and Block landed breathlessly beside them.

'The rest of us are still after Sariel, boss. He's headed out to sea,' puffed Block. 'What do you want us to do?' He cast a glance at Piccolo, who was bright-eyed with wonder at the sudden abundance of angels in his life.

'Shouldn't he be napping by now?' he wondered.

'Yep, in a minute,' said Dave, and he gave

them instructions. Some Gypsies were to return to the house. The other bundles would be waking up. The rest would keep looking for Mr Tompkins, whose real name was Sariel.

While Dave was talking to the bikers, Annabelle nudged Piccolo and whispered slowly and importantly, '*The cheese. It Mystified you*,' and she mimed nodding off to sleep.

Piccolo finally understood. He yawned extravagantly, mumbled some nonsense and pretended to sleep. Block was satisfied that things were in order.

Dave was finishing his speech.

'We can't let this one get away, boys. He doesn't look like a lot, but he's very dangerous and very important. I've been after him for eons.'

Block and Flathead flew off to deliver Dave's instructions.

'Are you *awake*, Piccolo?' asked Dave. Piccolo lifted an eyelid slightly.

'Come on. Up you get. Time to go.' Piccolo

stood up sheepishly and looked at Annabelle, who looked sheepish herself.

'You people have some explaining to do,' said Dave. The remains of poor Pootles burst into flames. They stood respectfully by her for a moment and watched her burn.

'I don't suppose she's fixable, Dave?' Annabelle asked.

He shook his head. 'No, luv. She's gone to the Great Garage.'

The fishermen were still fast asleep and there were no other folk about. Dave held Piccolo in his arms and flew up the cliff face. This was a much more pleasant trip, thought Piccolo, than his downward one. At the top they were greeted by Busstop. He ran around in tight little circles, yapping happily. Dave's big gleaming bike lay where he had dropped it to fly after Piccolo. He picked it up and brushed it off.

'Damn that demon! Look! A scratch!'

They all crowded on and rumbled home.

CHAPTER TEN
Head Hunting

Piccolo had a tight but comfortable ride wedged between Dave and Annabelle, with Busstop wrapped around his shoulders. He felt snug as a bug. A bug or two belonging to Busstop hopped onto Piccolo, but he was far too happy to be bothered. They chugged into Clearwater Bay, and then Pleasant Crescent. Mrs Jolly shrank behind a bush, scowling after them and scribbling in her watch book. At last they turned into Piccolo's driveway. It was nine o'clock in the morning. Piccolo had run away from home for three hours and twenty minutes, but it seemed much, much longer.

They were halfway along the driveway when a sudden commotion erupted from the direction of the house. Something flew low and fast towards them and close behind was a huge flying Gypsy. In an instant, Dave stopped the bike, reached into his pocket and flung something at a winged thing. It squealed briefly then thudded onto the drive, sliding across the gravel to their feet. The chasing Gypsy, Blossom, landed and stood over a crumpled demon. Piccolo remembered to be asleep.

'Thanks, boss. Good shot with the cheese. They're waking up all over the place. Better get back and find a new bag for this one.' He turned to go, then added, 'Ah, a bloke rang, Annabelle. Wanted to buy the goats. I told him they were sold already. Thing is, we're a bit fond of the goats ourselves. And we were thinking, some of us . . .' There was shouting from the house. 'Get it quick!' a deep voice shouted.

'We'll talk about it later,' suggested Annabelle, and Blossom hurried away.

Dave drove around the Mystified demon. Piccolo recognized it.

'That's Mrs Arnott. She's a cashier at the bank. Wow, she's a demon cashier. Are all those bundles full of demons?'

'I'm afraid so,' said Annabelle, 'and all from the Dependable Bank. A whole nest of demons were there, having a sausage sizzle and plotting

evil. I think I'll be moving my money to the Reliable Bank tomorrow.' As they reached the house she said, 'Better shoosh now, Piccolo.'

Two Gypsies were wrestling a shrieking demon back into its bag by the front steps. Annabelle sidestepped this unpleasantness as she carried 'sleeping' Piccolo inside.

Everywhere bundles were being reMystified, retied, and stacked on the verandah. When this was done, all the Gypsies, except for Dump and Dave, left to join the search for Mr Tompkins. Dump stood guard over the demon bundles. Dave found Piccolo and Annabelle in Piccolo's bedroom. He closed the door and sat down on the bed and looked from one to the other.

'Now,' he said, 'it's time for some explaining.'

'I kept meaning to tell you, Dave, that Piccolo is an Angelspotter,' blurted Annabelle, 'and I know you wouldn't dob him in to the Authorities, but . . .'

'Annabelle, I *am* an Authority!' he interrupted grimly. Piccolo was stunned. A dreaded Angel Authority was sitting on the end of his own bed.

'Yes, but you're a nice one and always have been.' She turned to Piccolo and explained. 'Dave wasn't just looking for diamonds in my jungle. He was my Inspector while I was there. He's a real softy. He wouldn't send you to Angelspotters' Academy, would you, Dave?' She wrapped her arms around Piccolo protectively.

'You're putting me in a difficult position here, Annabelle,' said the grizzled Angel Authority, twisting his beard. 'Angelspotters' Academy is a bit boring and strict, I'll admit,' said Dave, 'but it exists for good reasons—to keep you away from the likes of Demon Sariel for one thing.'

He lowered his great bushy eyebrows and looked intensely at Piccolo. 'If that demon *did* pick you for an Angelspotter, and if he *gets away* . . . the bad guys won't stop until they catch you.' He leant forward and took Piccolo's hands. 'And believe me, that would be a lot worse than a boring angel boarding school.'

'Why, what would the demons do to me?' he shuddered.

'They'd turn you into an Angelspotting Demon, horns and all. I've seen it before. Not pretty. Then they'd use you to spot angels, catch them and take them, you know, down there,' he added, pointing through the floor. 'And I don't mean your kitchen.'

Suddenly, despite all Annabelle's warnings, Angelspotters' Academy sounded like a very sensible place to be. But he asked, 'Can't Annabelle protect me here?'

'I don't know. Can you, Annabelle?'

'Of course I can, Dave. With my life.'

'Geez . . . I don't know . . .' Dave was pacing up and down the room, deep in thought, deciding Piccolo's future.

'Are all Demon Hunters bikies?' asked Piccolo, hoping to delay a decision.

'Sorry? What? No. They can be anything. Last time we were a ladies' lawn bowling team, clean and white but deadly to demons. Pretty good at bowls too,' he smiled, 'and we ate a lot of sponge cake.

'When we'd used up that disguise we bought bikes and grew beards. Grub thought up the cheese thing. We've been after these bank demons for years. We'll have to find a new disguise when all this is over. We'll miss those big bikes, I can tell you,' he added wistfully, and chuckled. 'But I've had enough cheese for a while, to tell the truth.' He stood and began pacing about the room.

'We've got to finish this job first, though. If we can't get Demon Sariel you'd better pack for the Angelspotters' Academy, Piccolo—which you should be doing anyway. I don't know. Can't sit here any longer, though. I'm going hunting. Wish me luck.'

Piccolo sincerely did as Dave strode outside.

Piccolo spent the rest of the day in his bedroom, pretending to be Mystified, and wondering what life would be like as a horned demon, or at Angelspotters' Academy. Occasionally a bike would thunder down the drive. Annabelle would run outside for news, and return to Piccolo shaking her head.

'Don't worry, luv. These are the best Demon Hunters in all the worlds. Dave hand-picked them himself.'

The short winter day ended. Dave, Brick, and Blossom had not come back but most of the other Gypsies had returned, giving up the search until morning. They sat about in small groups muttering and pulling at their beards. A night ago they had been silly as beans, full of cheese and doing dangerous stunts.

Piccolo could not face the cheese-free fruit selection Annabelle had brought him on a tray. He tried to go to sleep but his mind whirled and reeled and plummeted with the day's happenings.

Eventually he slid into another awful hunted dream, where he rode a bright pink motor scooter from bank to bank, hiding, riding, and hiding again. A swarm of black-winged bank cashiers pursued him into the mouth of a giant flounder, then a posse of stern Angel Authorities chased him out again and into a picnic shelter. They roared at him. The roar turned to cheering. Piccolo realized he was awake, and the cheering was real and coming from the driveway. He hurried over to the window. The last three bikes were back! Dave, Brick, and Blossom were surrounded by large joyful Gypsies. Busstop leapt up and down, yapping. Gypsies slapped each other's backs and there was some belly bouncing. Brick held a bundle above his head. Out of it slid a damp, bedraggled thing. It plopped onto the gravel and its wings twitched a little. It was Sariel, the dangerous Mr Tompkins, captured and bound.

Annabelle burst into the bedroom. 'Did

They didn't like the look of him.

you see? They got him!' Piccolo let himself be smothered with pink teary kisses. 'Oh, what a relief!'

When she finally let him go, Piccolo dried himself a little and asked, 'Does this mean I can stay here with you?'

'We'll have to see what Dave says, but I think so.'

'Where did they find Mr Tompkins?'

'On a prawn trawler way out at sea. He'd come up in a net, half dead. The prawning people were about to throw him back. They didn't like the look of him,' she laughed. 'Dear, oh dear. I feel so much better now, and so should you, Piccolo.'

He did. His queasiness had gone, and a powerful tiredness like a king size mattress fell on him.

'Now, you get some sleep. And no running away in the night?'

'No, Annabelle,' said Piccolo happily.

CHAPTER ELEVEN
Goodbyes

Piccolo woke late the next morning. A weak winter sun trickled past the curtains.

There was movement outside, and motorbikes kicked into life. Piccolo shook off the last of his dreams and ran to the window. Two dozen big bikes, laden with large Gypsies and lumpy bundles, were lined up in formation on the driveway. Two of the bikes had a goat each. Dave and Annabelle stood nearby.

'They're going! I have to say goodbye!'

He jumped into some slippers and raced

downstairs, putting on a dressing gown as he went. He stopped on the cold front steps, suddenly feeling silly and small. Annabelle trotted over to him.

'Am I still Mystified?' Piccolo whispered.

'No, it's all right. They're just some friendly bikers taking bundles to the tip, aren't they?' Annabelle winked.

'Will they really just dump them at a tip?'

'That would be nice, but too easy. No, they go to a demon re-education school. Most of them were angels once, you know. They'll be reminded of who they once were.' The boy and his guardian walked over to the burbling bikes. Piccolo shook twenty-four big hands.

'Thanks for havin' us,' they beamed. 'Beaut place you've got here,' they grunted. 'Hope we've cleaned up properly.' None of them mentioned the running away, or the demon hunt, or poor dead Pootles. Piccolo felt a bit guilty as he patted the goats goodbye, but they seemed happy in their new helmets.

The pack rode away at last with a deafening roar. One bike remained.

Dave joined Annabelle and Piccolo on the driveway.

'We've still got some serious thinking to do before I go,' Dave grumbled into his beard. They walked silently into the kitchen and sat down at

the table. Busstop joined them. Dave looked very serious. Piccolo was nervous again. His whole future would be decided in the next few moments: dull, strict, regimented Angelspotters' Academy, or his home, beautiful Holywell, with his eccentric, irritating, embarrassing, noisy, silly great-aunt? The Academy would at least be safe, and he was not afraid of discipline, and he knew he was a bit dull anyway. But it had been clear, sitting on his bed with angel arms around him, where he wanted to be. He was loved and cared for at Holywell. And he loved his angel too, mostly, some of the time.

'If my boss knew what I was about to say, I'd be in a lot of trouble,' he sighed at last. Annabelle grinned as he fiddled with his beard. 'You know the risks if you stay here, Piccolo?' Piccolo nodded. 'Then it looks like we all have some serious secrets to keep now.'

Annabelle bounced from her chair and wrapped her arms around Dave.

'Thank you, thank you, thank you. I won't let anything happen to him,' and she tried to find a clear space on his face to kiss.

'Meanwhile,' he continued, 'we'll have to boost security here. I've had a chat with Busstop here, and he's happy to move in, and bring his fleas too.'

Busstop yipped in agreement. 'He's a bit on the short side, but don't underestimate Busstop. He knows your little secret, but he won't breathe a word, will you, lad?'

'Yip, arf!'

Dave sighed. 'And us Gypsies are going to be deep-sea fishermen. We'll trade in our cheese for chips, and get even fatter! Hah!

'Your demon bank manager was headed out to an evil demon ship, he tells us. So a-sailing we shall go, me hearties, searching the briny seas. Arr.'

Talk of searching the seas reminded Piccolo of his own doomed plan to find his parents. He sagged, and looked at his hands. Dave seemed to read his mind.

'And while we're out there, Piccolo, we'll keep an eye out for your folks.'

Piccolo swelled with gratitude. 'Can I show you something before you go?' he asked.

It was a little crowded around the perch pond with tubby Annabelle, bulky Dave, and Busstop.

'This is Piccolo's special place, Dave,' said Annabelle respectfully.

'It sure is beautiful. There's a little bit of heaven in here, mate,' said Dave.

'When the water's warm, the perch like to nibble your toes. It's too cold now,' Piccolo explained.

'Can I try?' asked Dave. Piccolo said of course. Dave took off his boots, probably for the first time in months.

'Whooo! Sorry. Even I can smell that,' he

apologized. 'Ahhh, that's nice,' he sighed as he slid his hairy feet into the pond.

Piccolo was concerned for the health of his fish. But instead of turning belly up, they frolicked about Dave's hairy feet, their eyes wide with delight. Piccolo took off his slippers and carefully dipped his feet in. The water was warm. Annabelle joined them. They sat in silence enjoying the warmth and the tickling and nibbling. Busstop slipped in entirely, and paddled happily about.

'If I'm an Angelspotter, why can't I spot them?' asked Piccolo after a while. 'Good ones, I mean.'

'You spotted me,' Annabelle corrected him, 'and I'm a good one.'

'Yes, but only because you flew into the pear tree in broad daylight.'

Dave thought this was very funny, laughing until she dug him in the ribs.

'I was a bit rusty after a long time in the jungle, as well you know, David Fairfeather,' she huffed.

'I meant, why can't I see the golden glow? None of the Gypsies glowed.'

'No one can see the Gypsies glow. Demon Hunters have to be extra careful. We're glow-proofed,' explained Dave. 'OK, Piccolo, look at me and tell me if you notice anything.'

Piccolo looked at Dave. He saw a big hairy man who could comfortably lose twenty kilos. He saw a grizzly beard flecked with grey and bits of cheese and crackers. He saw heavy, shaggy eyebrows and sheltering under them were his clear grey eyes. Or were they blue? It seemed to Piccolo that they were changing colour as he looked. Yes, they were now unmistakably clear blue, and sparkling.

'Your eyes . . .' said Piccolo dreamily, '. . . and your beard is shrinking . . . and your wings . . .' He stood up and stepped back to get a better view. The scruffy overweight biker had gone, along with all the leather and studs. Dave was clothed in white and glowing with light, silver

The scruffy overweight biker had gone.

and gold, his white hair cascading and wings shining brightly. Piccolo was dumbfounded.

'Is that still you, Dave?' he wondered.

'Yep. Still me, the real me.'

'Then . . . then am I Angelspotting you?'

'Yes, you are. Well—I'm helping you a bit, but you'll see lots of my type with some practice.'

'Show off,' said Annabelle, pretending to be unimpressed. 'You're too gorgeous for your own good.'

The golden vision suddenly became a hairy biker again. He gave Annabelle a big squeeze, stood up abruptly and put on his smelly boots.

'I'd better get going before I get all teary.'

The perch swam farewell circuits of the pond. Busstop shook himself dry as Piccolo and Annabelle dried and dressed their feet too.

They walked arm in arm back to the house. Dave promised to let Piccolo know if they had news of his parents, but only if he promised to take great care of his secret, for all their sakes.

He made Annabelle promise to find a new, less controversial hobby. They reached the front drive. There was another big machine parked next to Dave's. It was a deep blue-green with a sleek sidecar, all sparkling new.

'Oh look! A spare bike and sidecar! What a surprise!' said Dave beaming. 'They're for you two, in memory of Pootles and Little Toot.'

Piccolo was thrilled and horrified at the same time. The thought of Annabelle driving this huge machine . . . No, he couldn't think about it.

'The keys are in her. Give her a whirl.'

'Fabulous, fabulous! Thank you, Dave!' Annabelle bounced on board in a flash and turned the key. The big motor purred. Piccolo picked up a shiny new helmet. It read 'Piccolo Grande' and fitted perfectly. He carefully climbed into the roomy sidecar. The seat was covered in soft blue leather.

Dave led the way down the driveway on his

bike and stopped at the gate. Annabelle followed smoothly.

'And this is as far as you go, my dear. Hide the keys, Piccolo, until she gets that licence. I'll be back.'

He rode away. On the corner, Mrs Jolly noted his passing.

Golden light enveloped the big man as he disappeared at the end of Pleasant Crescent. Piccolo blinked.

It's just the sun going down, he thought, and swallowed a great lump in his throat. Annabelle sighed.

'God bless that angel.'

Piccolo glanced at his own angel, sitting on the big bike next to him, and looked again. Was that a light shimmering around her, a golden one?

Annabelle started up their new machine again and motored slowly on to the street.

'Annabelle! Where are you going?'

'Well I can't turn this great lump around in the driveway, can I? Oh look. There's Mrs Jolly. I'll just give her a bit of a thrill.'

'No!' said Piccolo. 'NOOOOOoooooooo!'

About Stephen Axelsen

Born in Sydney a long time ago, Stephen has illustrated hundreds of children's stories and cartoon strips since 1974 and this is his fifth book as author and illustrator.

Stephen lives by the beach, watching the tides, near Byron Bay with his wife, Jennifer, and two big children, Lauren and Harlee. They share their house with a dog named Oscar, a cat called Willow, and their budgie, Trippy. When not illustrating or writing, Stephen might be found gardening, walking Oscar, or reading until he falls asleep. He also hunts cane toads on summer nights, but not for pleasure!

Acknowledgements

I would like to thank Heather again and Zoe, and my wife Jennifer for the music in my life.